D1530213

Bret and Grandma's Trip!

Level 1E

Written by Isabel Crawford
Illustrated by Sue King
Reading Consultant: Betty Franchi

About Phonics

Spoken English uses more than 40 speech sounds.
Each sound is called a *phoneme*. Some phonemes relate
to a single letter (d-o-g) and others to combinations
of letters (sh-ar-p). When a phoneme is written down,
it is called a *grapheme*. Teaching these sounds, matching
them to their written form, and sounding out words for
reading is the basis of phonics.

Early phonics instruction gives children the tools to sound
out, blend, and say the words without having to rely on
memory or guesswork. This instruction gives children the
confidence and ability to read unfamiliar words, helping
them progress toward independent reading.

About the Consultant

Betty Franchi is an American educator with a Bachelor's Degree in Elementary and Middle Education as well as a Master's Degree in Special Education. Betty holds a National Boards for Professional Teaching Standards certification. Throughout her 24 years as a teacher, she has studied and developed an expertise in Phonetic Awareness and has implemented phonetic strategies, teaching many young children to read, including students with special needs.

Reading tips

This book focuses on consonant, consonant, vowel, consonant words.

Tricky and/or new words in this book

Any words in bold may have unusual spellings or are new and have not yet been introduced.

> **Tricky and/or new words in this book**
>
> **the what they**

Extra ways to have fun with this book

After the readers have finished the story, ask them questions about what they have just read.

What did Bret and Grandma do on their trip?
How did Bret and Grandma catch all the crabs in the end?

Make flashcards of the consonant, consonant, vowel, consonant words in this book. Ask the reader to say the words, sounding them out. This will help reinforce letter/sound matches.

If Grandma and Bret want to catch me, they'll have to get snappy!

A Pronunciation Guide

This grid highlights the sounds used in the story and offers a guide on how to say them.

s as in sat	**a** as in ant	**t** as in tin	**p** as in pig
i as ink	**n** as in net	**c** as in cat	**e** as in egg
h as in hen	**r** as in rat	**m** as in mug	**d** as in dog
g as in get	**o** as in ox	**u** as in up	**l** as in log
f as in fan	**b** as in bag	**j** as in jug	**v** as in van
w as in wet	**z** as in zip	**y** as in yet	**k** as in kit
qu as in quick	**x** as in box	**ff** as in off	**ll** as in ball
ss as in kiss	**zz** as in buzz	**ck** as in duck	

Be careful not to add an /uh/ sound to /s/, /t/, /p/, /c/, /h/, /r/, /m/, /d/, /g/, /l/, /f/ and /b/. For example, say /ff/ not /fuh/ and /sss/ not /suh/.

Bret and Grandma
go on a trip.

Bret and Grandma stop.
Grandma takes a lazy nap.

Bret goes for a jog and a swim.

Bret and Grandma
spot a crab.

They trap it in a box.

But **the** crab jumps from
the box. Darn!

Quick! Can Bret grab the crab?

Will Grandma grab the crab?

Bret and Grandma cannot
grab the crab!

The crab jumps back in. Plop!

Bret is sad. **What** a loss.

Bret is sad. **What** a loss.

Do not fret! Grandma has a net.

Bret and Grandma
get lots of crabs!

What a trip!

OVER 48 TITLES IN SIX LEVELS
Betty Franchi recommends...

Other titles to enjoy from Level 1

Bad Rat
978 1 84898 747 0

The Best Gift
978 1 84898 750 0

Clint and Grant Play I-Spy
978 1 84898 752 4

Some titles from Level 2

Wish Fish
978 1 84898 755 5

Chuck and Duck
978 1 84898 756 2

Pink Bunny
978 1 84898 760 9

Let's go to the Swings
978 1 84898 759 3

Some titles from Level 3

Bart's Go-Cart
978 1 84898 768 5

Queen Ella's Feet
978 1 84898 764 7

Puff Flies
978 1 84898 765 4

The Pop Duet
978 1 84898 767 8

An Hachette Company
First Published in the United States by TickTock, an imprint of Octopus Publishing Group.
www.octopusbooksusa.com

Copyright © Octopus Publishing Group Ltd 2013

Distributed in the US by
Hachette Book Group USA
237 Park Avenue, New York NY 10017, USA

Distributed in Canada by
Canadian Manda Group
165 Dufferin Street, Toronto, Ontario, Canada M6K 3H6

ISBN 978 1 84898 751 7

Printed and bound in China
10 9 8 7 6 5 4 3 2 1